Venezuelan Heritage

Celebrating Diversity in My Classroom

By Tamra B. Orr

21st Century Junior Library

Published in the United States of America by
Cherry Lake Publishing
Ann Arbor, Michigan
www.cherrylakepublishing.com

Reading Adviser: Cecilia Minden, PhD, Literacy expert and children's author

Photo Credits: ©klemen cerkovnik/Shutterstock, cover; ©Paolo Costa/Shutterstock, 4; ©Punchalit Chotikasatian/Shutterstock, 6; ©Sonja70/Shutterstock, 8; ©Shane H. Wilder/Shutterstock, 10; ©MarioA/Shutterstock, 12; ©Ildi Papp/Shutterstock, 14; ©nehophoto/Shutterstock, 16; ©FOTOGRIN/Shutterstock, 18; ©ekler/Shutterstock, 20

Library of Congress Cataloging-in-Publication Data
Name: Orr, Tamra, author.
Title: Venezuelan heritage / Tamra B. Orr.
Description: Ann Arbor : Cherry Lake Publishing, 2018. | Series: Celebrating diversity in my classroom | Includes bibliographical references and index.
Identifiers: LCCN 2018003322 | ISBN 9781534129085 (hardcover) | ISBN 9781534130784 (pdf) | ISBN 9781534132283 (pbk.) | ISBN z781534133983 (hosted ebook)
Subjects: LCSH: Venezuela–Juvenile literature.
Classification: LCC F2308.5 .O77 2018 | DDC 987–dc23
LC record available at https://lccn.loc.gov/2018003322

Cherry Lake Publishing would like to acknowledge the work of the Partnership for 21st Century Skills. Please visit *www.p21.org* for more information.

Printed in the United States of America
Corporate Graphics

CONTENTS

The official name of Caracas is Santiago de Leon de Caracas.

Vivid Venezuela

Venezuela is in northern South America. Venezuela is twice the size of California. Just over 30 million people live in Venezuela. The capital city is Caracas.

Over the past few years, millions of Venezuelans have **fled** their country. Increased violence, lack of jobs, and food shortages have driven them away. In 2017, the number of **refugees** doubled. Many refugees went to neighboring South American countries. A large number moved to the United States. They have settled in Florida, Texas, California, and New York.

Venezuela has more than 1,400 bird species.
Its national bird is the Troupial.

Bienvenido a mi casa!

The people in Venezuela speak Spanish. English is also common, especially in stores and businesses. French and Latin are taught in high school, and Italian is common. Throughout the country, more than 40 languages can be heard. *Bienvenido a mi casa* is how someone might say "Welcome to my house!"

Venezuela has more than 25,000 species of orchids.

Many Spanish **dialects** are spoken throughout the country. In Caracas, people speak a special form of Spanish. It blends Portuguese, African, and Italian words. In remote areas, the language is very different. It can be almost impossible for others to understand!

Make a Guess!

Venezuela is one of the most **mega-diverse** countries in the world. This means it is home to most of the planet's wildlife species. There are only 16 other countries that are mega-diverse. And a number of species are found only in Venezuela. Why do you think so much wildlife is found here? What things are necessary to make it a mega-diverse country?

On Christmas, many Venezuelan families roller skate to church.

Religions Old and New

Almost three-quarters of Venezuelans are Roman Catholic. Others identify as either Protestant or as **atheists**. In Caracas, there are small communities of Jews and **Muslims**. The capital city has a large **mosque**.

A small number of Venezuelans follow an old religion called **Santeria**. It began in Cuba centuries ago. But the religion is

The first people to follow Santeria were told to become Catholic. They hid their beliefs by using Catholic saints to represent their gods.

still practiced in some South American countries. In the last few years, more Venezuelans have returned to this faith. A number of shops sell roosters, goats, and other animals used in religious **rituals**.

Tajadas are eaten in other Caribbean countries. These countries are Nicaragua, Colombia, Honduras, and Panama.

Tajadas and Arepas

It looks like a banana and peels like a banana. But it does not taste like a banana. What is it? It is a **plantain**. In Venezuela, plantains are one of the most popular side dishes. Known as *tajadas*, plantains can be sliced, salted, and fried like french fries. They can also be topped with honey as a sweet treat. Next to your tajadas, you might find an *arepas*. This is a Venezuelan sandwich

If someone invites you over for dinner, it is polite to arrive 30 minutes to one hour late.

made from corn cakes. Arepas can be baked or fried. Then they are filled with eggs, meat, or vegetables.

The country's national dish is *pabellon criollo*. Steak is slow cooked and shredded. Then it is added to a plate of rice and beans. Naturally, it comes with plantains on the side!

There has been a lack of meat, milk, coffee, and rice. Many Venezuelans must look for food.

Problems and Protests

Venezuela has problems that make life difficult for its people. Jobs are hard to find. Many people are poor. Food and medicine are in short supply. Crime is everywhere. Problems with government officials never end. **Protests** are common, and many of them have turned violent.

Venezuelans have also fled to Colombia.

This is why millions of Venezuelans have been leaving. They are heading for better lives elsewhere. The country's leaders are working to find solutions to their problems. Until then, refugees will continue to hope for the best for their homeland.

Think!

Venezuelan students can decide to attend school in the morning or the afternoon. When they get older, they can even choose to take night classes. Would you like to be able to do that? Which would you choose? Why?

GLOSSARY

atheists (AY-thee-ists) people who do not believe in any god

dialects (DYE-uh-lekts) ways of speaking in a particular area

fled (fled) ran away

mega-diverse (meg-uh-dih-VURS) having an extremely large number of wildlife species

mosque (MAHSK) a building where Muslims worship

Muslims (MUHZ-limz) people who follow a religion called Islam

plantain (PLAN-tayn) a tropical fruit that looks like a banana but is eaten cooked

protests (PROH-tests) events where people show they are against an idea, an act, or a way of doing things

refugees (ref-yoo-JEEZ) people seeking a safe place to live

rituals (RICH-oo-uhlz) actions or sets of actions that you repeat often

Santeria (san-TAIR-ee-uh) an old religion based on spirits

Venezuelan Words

arepas (uh-RAY-puhz) a sandwich made with baked or fried bread and then filled with sandwich ingredients

Bienvenido a mi casa! (bee-en-veh-NEE-doh AH MEE CAH-sah) "Welcome to my house!"

pabellon criollo (pah-BAY-ohn CREE-yo-yo) Venezuela's national dish of shredded steak with rice and beans and plantains on the side

tajadas (tuh-HAH-duhz) plantains that are sliced, salted, and fried or topped with honey

FIND OUT MORE

BOOKS

Murray, Julie. *Venezuela.* Minneapolis: Big Buddy Books, 2018.

Watson, Galadriel Findlay. *Angel Falls: The World's Highest Waterfall.* New York: AV2 by Weigl, 2014.

Willis, Terri. *Venezuela.* New York: Children's Press, 2013.

WEBSITES

Ducksters—Venezuela

www.ducksters.com/geography/country.php?country=Venezuela
Learn about the economy, history, and geography of Venezuela.

Multicultural Kid—Venezuela

https://multiculturalkidblogs.com/2017/12/04/fun-facts-about-venezuela-kids/
Discover unusual fun facts about Venezuela, especially for kids.

Science Kids—Country Facts: Venezuela Facts for Kids

www.sciencekids.co.nz/sciencefacts/countries/venezuela.html
Learn even more about Venezuela.

INDEX

ABOUT THE AUTHOR

Tamra Orr is the author of hundreds of books for readers of all ages. She graduated from Ball State University, but moved with her husband and four children to Oregon in 2001. She is a full-time author, and when she isn't researching and writing books, she writes letters to friends all over the world. Orr enjoys life in the big city of Portland and feels very lucky to be surrounded by so much diversity.